SAGE FINDS SUMMER

Patricia Gordon
WORD SANCTUARY 2021

Copyright © 2021 Patricia Gordon
All rights reserved

The characters and events portrayed in this book are fictitious. Any similarity to real persons, living or dead is coincidental and not intended by the author.

No part of this book may be reproduced, or stored in a retrieval system, or transmitted in any form or by any means, electronic, mechanical, photocopying, recording or otherwise, without express written permission of the publisher.

ISBN-978-1-7367578-1-9

Cover design by Kimberley Kaye
Library of Congress Control Number: 2021906862
Printed in the United States of America

Thanks to my mommy, Althea Spence, who helped birth Sage in me with that first pencil stroke we took with her hands over mine.

Praise For Sage

"When I felt upside down, Aunty told me to look around myself, open my eyes and see about someone else!" By the end of this story Sage fulfills the promise of her name. She gains wisdom when she learns that happiness comes from helping others along with another lesson in Patricia Gordon's remarkable book: We should help others from the kindness of our hearts, not because we expect to get something in return. Sage Finds Summer is a 5-star book young girls and boys will love.
- *Elizabeth Nunez, Ph.D.* is the award-winning author of ten novels and a memoir, and winner of an American Book Award and the Hurston Wright Legacy award, among others.

In this novelty chapter book, Sage DOES find a new summer as she navigates between grief and giving. With its uplifting prose and thoughtful extension guide, this read rings timeless. Gordon has crafted a faithful keepsake. Fabulous!
- *Teffanie Thompson,* award-winning author of DIRT

Try to be a rainbow in someone's cloud. – Aslan

Contents

Last Day Blues 1

Ice Cream With A Sprinkle
Of Words On Top 9

Friends Lost And Found 16

New Binky, New Home 27

Words I Need To Know 35

The Whos 38

Discussion Questions 39

Last Day Blues

"Like what, Sage?" Jorge asked. Just tell us one thing you're doing this summer!"

"Yeah! We told you our plans, why can't you tell us yours, Sage?" Aja challenged.

All around the sunlit classroom, children **devoured** happy flavors dipped in rainbow frostings. Small fans that failed against the late morning humidity, waved salty, sugary scents that met and **mingled** under the turned off lights. It was only an hour ago parents had unloaded bulky shopping bags for the end of the year party, transforming the study room into a feast space. When Ms. Kaye had instructed everyone to bring a favorite food, enough for two friends, the children got it! For once, hands didn't go up with questions. Ms. Kaye wished that first time, one time, direction had worked a little more often.

"It's my summer. I don't have to talk about it if I don't want to!" Sage Spencer snapped at her friends. She was glad the noisy room couldn't carry her voice to the next table. She dragged on her straw, barely tasting her juice. She had nothing else to say.

Despite the crunching and the music, the laughter and the talking, Sage managed to pick out bits of conversation that were all the same. She heard who was going where for the summer. Who was doing what, and who was having family visit from places she'd never heard of before.

Even Ms. Kaye couldn't look serious today. The boxes and gift bags that sat on her desk were from parents grateful for her help in making the fourth-graders shine over the past year. Curious to see what surprises they held, the students begged her to unwrap the crisp tissue paper, before she tucked them into her going home bag. But Ms. Kaye resisted their pleas. She said opening them at home would be her personal, official start of the summer celebration.

Jared circled the group table, arms out like the airplane that would fly him and his family to the **U.K.** for the Wimbledon tennis tournament. Barely moving out of his way before she was run over, Aja wrapped her arms around her shoulders as she anticipated her family's upcoming road trip.

"Our minivan's gonna be sooo packed for the ride to Nana's lakehouse in North Carolina! But when we get there," she paused with a smile, "we'll have lots of space to hike, fish, and do whatever we want!" she said dreamily.

Not about to be outdone by his friends, Jorge sputtered between two cream-filled cookies, "My sister's the best shooting guard on her college team. She's gonna help me make my jump shot even better!" After shoving in a third cookie, he pretended to land a 3- pointer in an imaginary basket, shouting, "Brooklyn Nets, here I come!"

Too busy making crowd-like *aahs and ohs* with hands cupped around his mouth, Jorge didn't notice the pasty black and white smears dotting his palms, now smudged on his jersey. His aim at an imaginary basket was much better than his real time aim with food! Sage abruptly pushed back from the table, annoyed by the scraping sound her chair made with the floor. She remembered just in time that when Jorge was excited and chewing food, someone close by was going to wear some of it!

Everyone had something to look forward to this summer, while Sage was missing the summer she already lost. She was mostly glad her friends had found theirs, though. *Mostly. I remember how awesome our summers used to be,* Sage thought, as her friends continued to out talk each other.

When Papa was alive, he planned the vacations and kept the **destinations** secret -- even from Mommy. No matter how much Sage and her brother Quinn tickled and **pestered** him with questions, Papa's lips stayed sealed.

For seven-year old Quinn and Sage, the last day of school used to be loaded with a suspense ready to burst by the time they got home. That's when Papa, eager to unload the secret himself, just had to reveal the name of the mysterious place. But tonight there would be no guessing games, tickles, or giggles around the dinner table. No "drum roll" with Papa and Quinn tapping their forks on their plates before the big reveal. Sage fidgeted with one of her dark springy braids and sighed, wishing school wasn't ending today.

The friends and school projects that filled the days over the past months helped her to not think about Papa. Well, not *that* much. But when it was time for her and Quinn to set the table for dinner, memories settled on her the way the lace tablecloth blanketed the round dinner table. And there were still nights Quinn needed reminding to put out three plates instead of four.

As far as Sage could see, this summer was going to be endlessly empty. There wouldn't be her father's deep humming to welcome the morning. Mommy couldn't say, "Go away, Carl!" between blushes when Papa pulled her from the stove for a dance. The more Sage thought about tomorrow and every day after, summer, and all the joy that came with it, died when Papa did. So before her friends nagged her with one more question that could bring on

tears, Sage sprang from her seat. It was only Jared's quick save that kept Jorge's milk from diving to the floor.

Ice Cream With A Sprinkle Of Words On Top

"I know you're table leader, Aja, but I'll do clean-up for you just this once," Sage offered, as if there would be another reason to clean up after today's bell.

Two hours and many bites later, the building's children poured into the sticky sunshine. Their voices deafened them to their teachers' wishes for a safe summer. With the passersby, school buses, and honking delivery trucks, this corner of Empire Boulevard was a noisier scene than usual. It seemed everything and everyone-- everyone but Sage, was pumped that today was the last day of school!

Whether it was a person or a machine, all moved faster than Sage, who dragged along the steamy, Brooklyn sidewalk. It didn't help that every step she took repeated *lost summer, lost summer.* She knew that Mommy and her brother waited for her in the generous shade of the tree Quinn had claimed as theirs. She also knew that on the walk home they would see the same sights they saw yesterday, the day before that and last week. So why hurry?

"Last one to Mommy is a rotten egg!" Quinn yelled behind his sister, hoping to scare her. "I'm gonna choose our treat spot today, Sage, cuz I'm gonna beat you!" And then Quinn dashed in Mommy's direction, the back of his sneakers lifting high off the pavement.

He was teasing his sister about the new family **tradition** of the after-school treat. When the next day was a Saturday or a holiday, Mommy took them to Ivan's Ice Cream Igloo, or to the playground where the sizzle of the sprinkler greeted them at the gate. **Ordinarily**, the 'Treat Spot Challenge' was too good a dare for Sage to pass up, and Quinn would've gotten the race he wanted. But neither the hope of a creamy delight or the thrill of a glide on the swings quickened her pace--not today.

Mommy had to lift Sage's face to meet her gaze, once she joined them under the sheltering tree. Strangely, Mommy's **jasmine** scented hug, which **remedied** most ills, could only touch the top of Sage's misery today. "Hey, long chin mek' eyes dim," Mommy teased.

That was Mommy's **particular** way of saying Sage would miss the "wonder moments" of the day, if her eyes were shaded in sadness. Mommy had spent part of her childhood in the country of **Jamaica**, and was loaded with countless expressions that gift wrapped wisdom in humor. When she shared them in the rhythm rich speech of her parents, Sage and Quinn repeated them, or at least they *tried* to, as they guessed their meanings between giggles.

But Sage said nothing, as if she didn't hear it. Soon Mommy's eyes, hot cocoa hued, like Sage's, were inches from hers.

"Want to tell me about it?" Mommy asked.

Sage turned her head away, slightly amazed at the almost empty street. For a second, she wondered exactly when the other kids and families had disappeared. But

Mommy was waiting for an answer.

I hate that everything's different… I wish it were last year when Papa was still alive and we were a whole family again… I wish, I wish… Sage shouted in her head.

"No Mommy." She said with a sigh. "Just bored." Of course, Mommy knew more than Sage was saying, but she let it go--for now. Not to mention, Quinn was slowing down his victory laps around the tree; a sign he was ready to get "treat spot" moving.

It was a treat just *stepping* into Ivan's Ice Cream Igloo after the six-block walk in the early afternoon heat. Many of Sage and Quinn's schoolmates were already gathered outside the frosted door of the cozy shop. They slooped the top *and* the bottom of their cones, trying to stay ahead of the 90 degree day's attempts to steal the precious drops from them.

Quinn ran in and gave Mr. Ivan a fist bump while asking about the flavor of the day. Then he read all the names of the 15 **fantastic** cone creations on the board- one- at- a- time. Sage rolled her eyes and sighed whenever her brother went through this **ritual**. They all knew what he was going to do. After slowly reading through the list, he still was going to ask Mr. Ivan to make the crunchiest "Coconut Crunch" cone there ever was, with exactly four M&Ms on top!

Sage impatiently tapped his shoulder and swiftly stepped ahead of him. "Mr. Ivan, I'd like the Peachy Lychee cone, please," she said.

"Coming right up, Sage!" Mr. Ivan winked as he **wielded** his scoop with a superhero flourish. Captive eyes were glued to his gloved hands, as he worked his cone-creating magic. Forgetting where he was in his **recitation**, Quinn shrugged his shoulders and started all over again with the first flavor on the list. Then Mommy did that "Shuri - like" thing again, impressing and unnerving Sage, at the same time.

Ice Cream with a Sprinkle of Words On Top

Friends Lost And Found

"Sage, did I ever tell you what my aunty used to call a day like this?"

"*Hot?*" Sage answered. If there was a moment she totally was not feeling one of Mommy's, 'When I was a girl in Jamaica' stories,' this was it! But she knew better than to say *that*.

"Well, whenever I had a day when I felt upside down, aunty told me to look around myself, open my eyes, and see about someone else!" Making her point with a squeeze of Sage's shoulder, Mommy leaned in closer. "You know, you can see much more when you take your eyes off yourself, Sage."

I hate when she does that-- telling me what's in my own head! Sage thought. *And how in the world does she expect me to figure out some crazy aunty saying?* Sage looked at her softening ice cream not knowing where to lick first. She was distracted by Jamaican aunts she never met and the Papa who wouldn't be home when she got there. *Juuust great, now I can't even concentrate on my cone*, she almost said aloud as she mentally **tallied** her list of problems. But catching Quinn's long look at her cone while he waited for Mr. Ivan to produce a fresh tin of Coconut Crunch from the freezer, motivated Sage to get to licking.

She was thinking so hard she didn't stop to pet Mr. Rodriguez's beagle on the walk home. She barely waved at Mrs. Goodstein's twins who yelled, "Hi Sage, hi Quinn, oh and hi, Mrs. Spencer!" from across the street. And Sage would've walked past the red truck in eye-catching yellow lettering declaring, "Don't Dropit Delivery," if Mommy hadn't said, "Someone's moving in."

Sage looked up in time to see two men in shirts the

same color as the truck, backing out of its rear door. They easily lifted a couch between them and stopped to speak to a towering man who pointed to the entrance of the apartment building. It took a few more blinks for Sage to notice the girl standing behind him.

This girl, who looked to be about her age, crouched as if trying to hide in the man's great shadow. She was wiping her eyes and clinging to his hand. After a few seconds, Sage focused again on the now soggy, pointy tip of her cone.

But Quinn was **fascinated!** He had already memorized the details of the wheels, planning the colored pencils he'd use to draw them, the minute he got back to his room. Quiet for once, he eased to the opening the men had come from, looking over his shoulder to make sure his sister and mother were busy making friends.

"Quinn! You can't just stick your big head in there! Come back here!" He felt, as his sister jerked him away from his goal. He had been foot close to making it up the ramp that would've taken him into the **cavernous** world of the truck.

"This way," Mommy said, nudging her son and daughter toward the strangers. "We have neighbors to make!" Smiling and nodding, Mommy and Mr. Valdez, as he said his name was, shared introductions and handshakes. Sage did her best to **imitate** Mommy, stretching her hand towards the girl, with what she hoped was a friendly smile. But unlike the adults' hellos, this wasn't going right.

"Hi, I'm Sa…" Sage's words trailed off then stopped. Confused, Sage looked from the girl to her father. She was sure she had copied Mommy to a "T," but did a quick mental check anyway to make sure. *Did I look her in the eye? Check. Did I put out my hand? Check. I know I smiled. Check. Not my greatest, but it'll pass.* Because instead of the smiles that come with first meetings, this one was met with tears.

"You have to forgive my daughter, Robyn," Mr. Valdez said while trying to pull her in front of him. "It's been a hard day, well year for her--for us, since **Hurricane Maria** destroyed our home. We-- my family and neighbors, have all had to take care of each other. I'm afraid Robyn is already missing her *mamita*, **abuelo**, and her best **amiga**."

Sage remembered learning these words from Senora Angora, the Spanish teacher, at school. She understood that not only did a **calamity** force Robyn to come to a strange place, but she had to come without her mother, grandfather and best friend. Sage recalled how she felt a few months ago having to leave Papa in that awful hospital room.

Nothing in that room was anything like him, especially the silence. It wasn't total, but interrupted by the beeping machine with tubes coming out of it and going into Papa. Sage had wondered if the beeps counted the breaths Papa was taking, or if they were **tolling** the breaths he had left. She knew if he were well and able to speak, he'd never have this scary ticking filling his space. No, Papa would've been singing to his favorite **Al Green** or **Bob Marley** playlists. When Mommy knew it was time to tell the children he'd never be coming home, Sage cried that day and many days after. Much like the way Robyn was crying now.

"I tell Robyn her mamita will join us as soon as she

can, and that in Brooklyn, she will make lots of amigas. But this first day, so far--" Mr. Valdez paused to shake his head, "is not so good. The doll Abuelo gave her before we left San Juan is missing. I hope somewhere between the truck, and the boxes upstairs, she will turn up."

What if I didn't have my Binky Bear those first few nights after Papa left us? Sage thought. Binky was her best loved teddy bear who never got tossed in the corner like her other stuff. He was either waiting for her on her bed, or **perched** on top of the latest book she was reading. No matter where she was in her room, Sage had Binky in view.

Listening to Mr. Valdez, she looked at Robyn again, getting an idea. Ms. Kaye always said the best ideas were the ones that turned into a way to help. "Come on, Q." Sage ordered as she tugged his arm. And this time she was running.

"Let's go!" She said louder, turning around to drag him from his headlight **examination**. "We have a doll to find!" Sage's idea meant a new adventure and maybe the chance to run, so Quinn's curiosity about the truck was gone--for now. They told Mommy where they were going and promised to stay together. Then the pair took off.

They searched near the mailboxes, **peered** inside the elevator, felt under the benches in the lobby and asked all the neighbors they saw if they had seen a doll. Sage and Quinn **inspected** every step and hallway of the 6-floor building. Out of breath and sweating by the time they returned to Mommy, Robyn's eyes told them the doll hadn't turned up in the now empty truck, either.

"You're back!" Mommy said. "You'll like to know the Valdez' will be living right below us. Maybe that'll make you two more quiet in the mornings," Mommy joked. "But say good-bye for now. Robyn and her dad have had a long day and they still have lots to do."

A few hours later in their 4th floor kitchen, Sage smoothed chocolate frosting on cupcake tops while Quinn licked the mixing spoon. Thinking about the afternoon, Sage didn't mean for her thoughts to move from her head to her mouth. "It must be hard saying good-bye to your home and your favorite doll all in one day."

"I'd say so," Mommy agreed. "Actually, poor Robyn and her dad have said many more good-byes than that."

Then Mommy paused for a moment.

"Sounds like someone isn't thinking so much about her boring summer anymore," she continued while looking directly at Sage. And in that moment, Mommy's weird words spoken at Mr. Ivan's made sense.

New Binky, New Home

"Take my eyes off myself, off myself," Sage repeated in a low voice only she could hear. Suddenly the box she and Papa had started packing months ago, came to mind. She and Quinn may not have been able to find Robyn's doll, but maybe she could find a doll for Robyn! Sage quickly wiped her hands and hurried to her closet.

Reverend Ben, their pastor, had said too many families in **Puerto Rico** and **Dominica** were barely surviving almost 2 years after Hurricane Maria. It was their responsibility as neighbors of the planet, to share what they could. Sage sank to the floor and **rummaged** through the half-filled box they were planning to give to the church. She couldn't believe this very day she had met a real family, just like those they were trying to help!

Hoping there was an old doll in the box that could cheer up Robyn, Sage slowed her frantic hands as a new thought began to settle in her. If she *really* wanted Robyn to know she understood how she felt, shouldn't she give her something that was *still* special to her? Sage sat quietly on her closet floor thinking this over, while again saying the words that had sent her to the closet in the first place.

From where she sat, she noticed Binky Bear against the cotton candy shaded pillow where she had left him that morning. Staring at him now, she thought of the countless nights he had listened in on her prayers with his fur drying her secret tears. Sage walked slowly to the bed picking him up, then holding him to her chest.

His left ear still held hints of Papa's musky cologne she missed so much. When Papa's stays in the hospital began to outnumber his days at home, Sage had brought the old bear to keep him company. She also hoped having Binky nearby would make Papa think of her.

"Mom, Mommy!" Sage cried, starting to run, then remembering the Valdez', walking back into the kitchen. "Do you think it would help Robyn if I gave her Binky? I don't know what her lost doll was like, but maybe he can be her 'feel better friend,' the way he's always been to me." Mommy put down the bowl she was drying at the sink and walked over to Sage. "Are you sure you're ready to part with Binky? You two are so close," Mommy said, touching the ends of Sage's braids.

"I think so," she spoke and nodded confidently. "I believe Robyn needs him more than I do right now," she stated, squinting the way Papa used to, as her ideas became clearer. Then she looked slowly up at her mother again. "What do you, think Mommy?"

"I think you are being a lot like our Heavenly Father, Sage. He gave us Jesus so we could know how much He loved us and how special we are to Him. That way we don't have to feel alone, no matter where we go, what happens to us or what we lose. I also know that your Papa would be so proud of you right now. So yes, I think Robyn will absolutely love Binky!" Mommy answered.

"But first, he needs to be cleaned up, before his meet-up!"

Using needle and thread, Mommy and Sage stitched a few ragged spots around Binky's ears and arms. Then a mini bubble bath in Sage's favorite soap and a few whirrs from the blow dryer, fluffed up his flattened fur. Even Quinn got in on the makeover. He decided the bear's neatly steamed bowtie needed one of his Cub Scout award pins for this special occasion. After a few more finishing touches, Binky's eyes and pin were sparkling.

"Can't call Binky 'old' anymore!" said Quinn when all was done. "Sure you still wanna give him away, Sagey? He looks and smells like new!" Sage and Binky walked with Mommy, who held the pan of cupcakes in one hand and Sage's free hand in the other. Quinn was already down the stairs, talking about what his prize should be for being the first one to the bell. As they got closer to their neighbors' door, Sage stopped. *Bedtime was gonna be different without Binky!* As this thought hit her, she didn't realize she was squeezing Mommy's hand, until Mommy squeezed back. *But it's a different I can do if I take my eyes off myself,* she determined, walking again.

"Another secret?" Mommy asked.

This time Sage's eyes happily looked up to meet Mommy's. "I saw Robyn after I took my eyes off myself-and then I saw a bunch of other things! That is so cool, Mommy!"

"It is!" Mommy agreed. "And while you were being a friend to your neighbor, someone was thinking about you! The youth director from church called and there's an open slot for camp, if you want it. Somebody who wants to remain **anonymous** did that just for you, Sage. All we have to do is get you packed and ready to get on that bus this weekend."

"Mommy can *noneemus* send me to camp too?" Quinn asked.

"Actually, Quinn, I think that a-no-ny-mous person really wanted to rescue you from your sister's bossiness for a couple weeks," Mommy said, turning to wink at her youngest. "Well Sage?"

"Nope! No thanks, Mommy," Sage said without having to think about it. "They need to send someone who's got nothing going on, cuz there's gonna be lots of

New Binky, New Home

summer happening right here! And who knows what *else* I'll find? And maybe Robyn will help me look too!"

Words I Need To Know:

1. <u>Anonymous</u> - A person whose name you don't know
2. <u>Calamity</u> (n) - A disastrous event
3. <u>Cavernous</u> (adj) - A space that's wide open and empty like a cave
4. <u>Charity</u> (n) - To give help to people who need it
5. <u>C'yan</u> Pronounced *ki/yahn* - Jamaican term meaning cannot
6. <u>Destination</u> (v) - The place that a person is traveling to
7. <u>Devour</u> (v) - To eat hungrily & quickly
8. <u>Dominica</u> (n) - Island nation in the Caribbean
9. <u>Examine</u> (v) - To look at something or someone very carefully
10. <u>Fantastic</u> (adj) - To be so good or so wonderful that it is hard to believe
11. <u>Fascinated</u> (vb) - When a person feels she or he must look or get close to someone or something
12. <u>Hurricane</u> (n) - A storm with violent winds and heavy rain that can destroy buildings, property and trees
13. <u>Hurricane Maria</u> (n) - A deadly hurricane that destroyed parts of Dominica, Jamaica and Puerto

Rico in September 2017
14. Imitate (v) - To do or say something in the exact way as it was shown to you
15. Jamaica (n) - Island nation in the Western Caribbean
16. Mingle (v) - To mix together
17. Particular (adj) - Relating to a person or a thing
18. Peer (v) - To look at carefully with concentration
19. Perch (vb) - To sit on the edge of something
20. Pester (vb) - To bother or annoy over and over again
21. Recitation (n) - Something that is said from memory
22. Remedy (n) - A cure for something
23. Ritual (n) - Something that is done the exact same way all the time
24. Rummage (v) - To search for something in a hurry and causing a mess
25. San Juan (n) - The capital or main city of Puerto Rico
26. Tally (vb) - To count or add
27. Tolled (vb) - When large clocks count the movement of time with a sound
28. Tradition (n) - A family's way of doing something
29. Unique (adj) - The only one of its kind
30. U.K. (n) - Abbreviation for the United Kingdom. This area in Western Europe includes Great Britain and Northern Island
31. Wielded (v) - To hold and use skillfully

The Whos:

- Al Green - African-American soul music singer
- Bob Marley - Jamaican Reggae poet and singer
- Shuri - Sister to the Black Panther from Marvel Comics who can sometimes read minds.

Sage Finds Summer Discussion Questions

1. Describe Sage's feelings early in the story. Why is she feeling this way? How is her state of mind different from that of her classmates?
2. Even though Papa died before we meet Sage, what are the ways she still feels very close to him?
3. What does Mommy's saying: "You can see much more when you take your eyes off yourself," mean? Why does she tell this to Sage? What is your opinion of Mommy's wisdom at this moment?
4. What happened to Robyn's home in Puerto Rico that caused her family to move to Brooklyn? Why is Sage able to connect with Robyn's sadness when she first meets her?
5. Why does Sage want to give Robyn her Binky Bear? What do you think about Sage's decision to give a stranger something she loves? What is something you own or a talent you have that could help someone going through a difficult time feel better?

6. Do you think Sage followed Mommy's advice that she would see more if she took her eyes off herself by the end of the story? Explain your answer.

For More Fun:

- Draw a picture or write a paragraph that could be a scene taking place after the story ends.
- Think of a saying that is used in your family, or create your own saying that you could share to help cheer someone up.
- Mommy reminds Sage that caring about someone's pain reflects God's love and is an act that would've made Papa proud. Find someone in your community who needs help and have your family or school, organize a plan to help them.
- Use a map to locate any of the places mentioned in the story: (Brooklyn, New York, U.K., Jamaica, Dominica, Puerto Rico) and discover 5 facts about that city or country. Cut out and/or draw pictures that support the facts you discovered. Then pretend you are a writer for a travel magazine. Write an article and include your pictures to convince someone to travel there!

Acknowledgements

Although Sage has been with me all my life, it was far more challenging than I ever imagined to get in touch with her and to release her from my head. I'm beyond grateful to the people who helped me give her voice, whether by encouragement or by rolling up their sleeves. There were others who gave her a face and presence, and there's one who made sure I had the room and the space to give her life. In other words, Sage might have been mine, but it took a team to bring her to the world.

To my oldest friend, Charmaine Walters, who's written hundreds of words with me from our junior high days, and who read these with the same exuberance and anticipation. Thanks Charm, for always being up for the ride with me.

Leilani Worrell, niece, educator and activist. You found time between championing for justice and honing your own excellence, to put on your editing cap for Aunty Pat. I'm so proud of you.

Wendy Douglas-Nathai, you know how to show up and stay late til it's done. You transformed my scribbles to a live website. Many thanks!

Kimberley Kaye, amazing how you visualized, then actualized Sage and her world! Thanks for taking this illustrative plunge with me. Your talents refreshed me in the moments my energy and confidence waned.

Iyeesha Cook, you opened up the possibility of authorship & self-publishing to me by your own dogged pursuit of it despite the obstacles. You are something else!

Judie Kelly, the Zoom lunch dates, the free therapy and the prayers! Girl… you know!

Peter Gordon, you survived your sister's bossiness and then told her to shine in everything she wanted to do. Thanks for inspiring Sage's Quinn.

Isabella Thomas-Gordon, your spirit and love for reading inspire me to want to keep writing for children like you.

Jeanette & Hal Gordon, your wellspring of understanding and wisdom, always available for me and all your children, is priceless.

Patrick Baxter, the Word Sanctuary, one fruit of the tree you fostered for me to create and explore in, couldn't have happened without your dedication to me and my dreams. Thank you!

And…praise the Lord, the giver of every good and perfect gift!

About The Illustrator

Florida based artist, Kimberley Kaye, has been drawing and painting professionally since 2003; exhibiting her work locally and internationally. She has had a passion for art from a very young age and gleans inspiration from nature's beauty, especially as it is found in her home country, Jamaica. Kimberley was briefly introduced to illustration while at the School of Visual Arts in New York City from 2006- 2008. Her illustrations in **Sage Finds Summer** are her first published works in a children's book. Experience more of Kimberley's art at www.artbykimberley.com.

About The Author

It was the gifts of an old-fashioned chalkboard and a "Nothing Book" that sparked the love of speaking to a page and seeing magic take place. An English teacher from Long Island, New York, Patricia pens from her Caribbean - American childhood as experienced in the cultural fabric of her Crown Heights, Brooklyn home. She writes "Sacred Scenewriting," creating theater from Biblical inspiration. **<u>Sage Finds Summer</u>** is her first children's book. Step into www.mywordsanctuary.net to learn more.

Made in the USA
Middletown, DE
04 July 2021